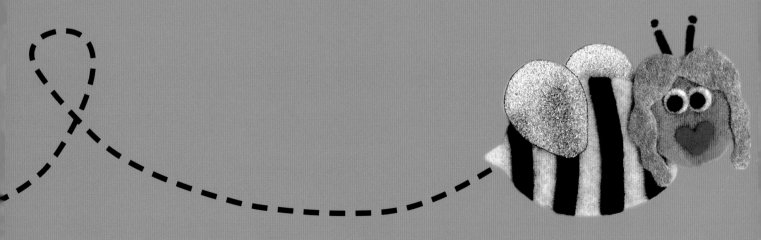

To my parents and family

Published by Little Linguists Press
The literary division of ChatterWorld, LLC

ChatterWorld and the multi-colored spiral logo are trademarks of ChatterWorld, LLC.

For information address: ChatterWorld, LLC, P.O. Box 169, Owings Mills, MD 21117, www.chatterworld.net

Library of Congress Control Number: 2006921160

ISBN-13: 978-0-9777085-0-5
ISBN-10: 0-9777085-0-0

Printed in China

ChatterWorld
playdates for little linguists™

My Numbers in Spanish

Mis números en español

Zakiyyah

Little Linguists Press

1 UNO (oo-noh)

Uno is one.
A rhythmic, wooden drum to
beat on just for fun.

un tambor (oon tahm-bohr)
one drum

2 **DOS** (dohs)

Dos is two.
Oh, no! Catch the balloons,
they're floating out of view.

dos globos (dohs gloh-bohs)
two balloons

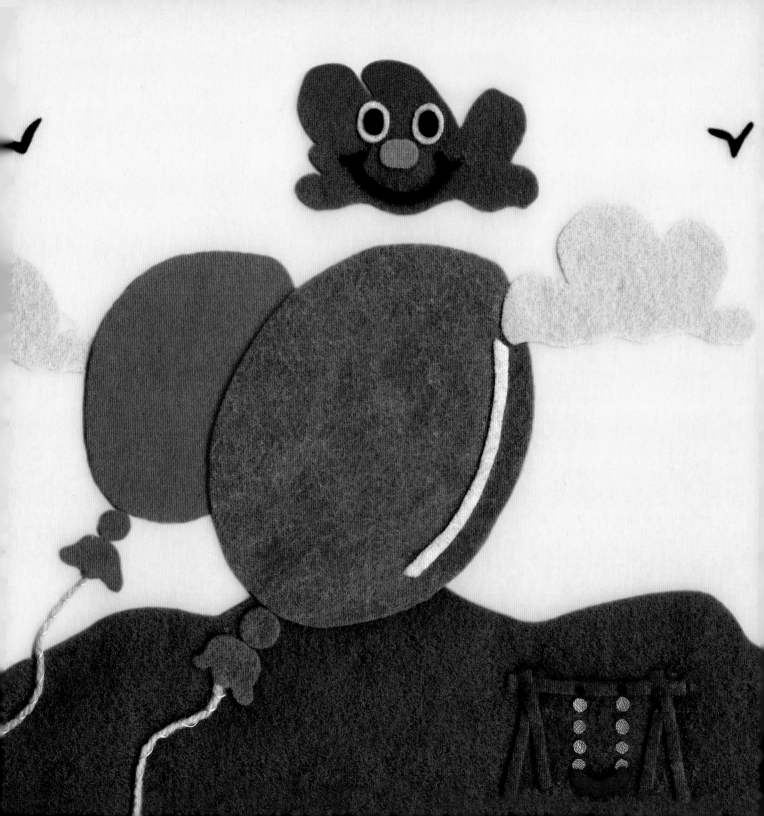

3

TRES (trehs)

Tres is three.
Listen to the lovely birds
singing in the tree.

tres pájaros (trehs pah-hah-rohs)
three birds

4 CUATRO (kwah-troh)

Cuatro is four.
Crunchy, red apples
eaten to the core.

cuatro manzanas (kwah-troh mahn-sah-nahs)
four apples

5

CINCO (seen-koh)

Cinco is five.
Count the bumble bees
buzzin' around the hive.

cinco abejas (seen-koh ah-beh-hahs)
five bees

6 SEIS (seys)

Seis is six.
Fun, colorful bouncy balls
to play with and to kick.

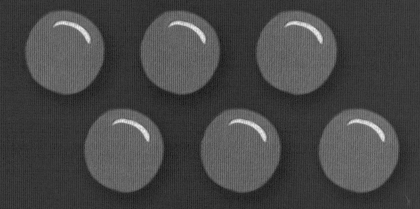

seis pelotas (seys peh-loh-tahs)
six balls

7

SIETE (see-yeh-teh)

Siete is seven.
Chunky, gooey cookies
pipin' hot from the oven.

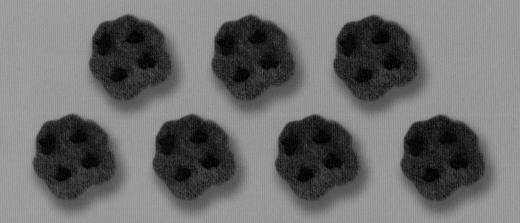

siete galletas (see-yeh-teh gah-yeh-tahs)
seven cookies

8

OCHO (oh-choh)

Ocho is eight.
Bunches of fragrant flowers
are growing along the gate.

ocho flores (oh-choh floh-res)
eight flowers

9

NUEVE (noo-weh-beh)

Nueve is nine.
Sweet, juicy strawberries are delicious and all mine.

nueve fresas (noo-weh-beh freh-sas)
nine strawberries

10

DIEZ (dee-yehs)

Diez is ten.
And, we're at the end.
Let's start with the
number *uno*, again.

diez números (dee-yehs noo-meh-rohs)
ten numbers

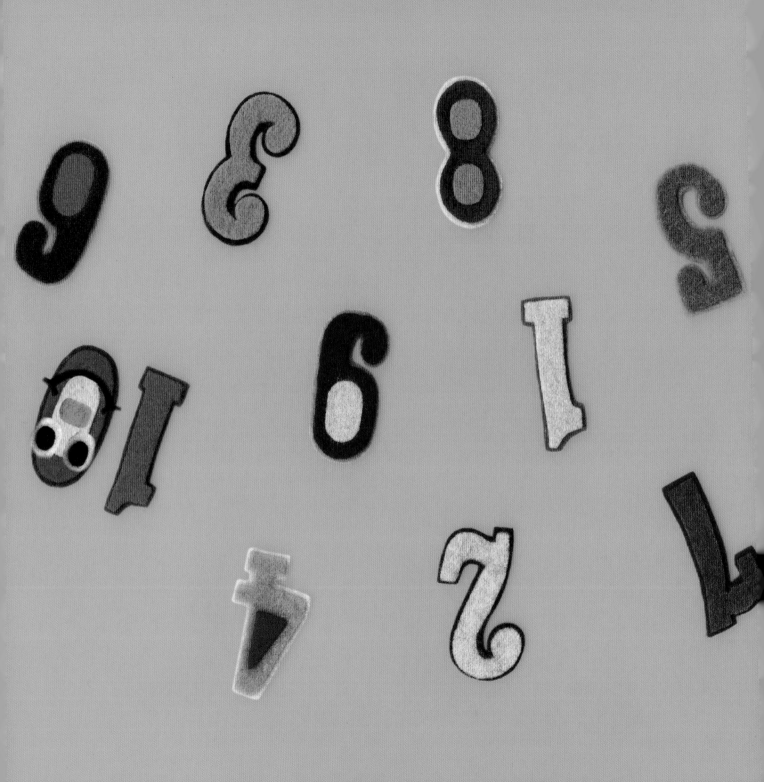

10 DIX (dees)

Dix is ten.
And, we're at the end.
Let's start with the
number *un*, again.

dix nombres (dees nohN-breh)
ten numbers

9 NEUF (nuhf)

Neuf is nine.
Sweet, juicy strawberries are delicious and all mine.

neuf fraises (nuhf frehz)
nine strawberries

8 HUIT (weet)

Huit is eight.
Bunches of fragrant flowers
are growing along the gate.

huit fleurs (weet fluhr)
eight flowers

7

SEPT (seht)

Sept is seven.
Chunky, gooey cookies
pipin' hot from the oven.

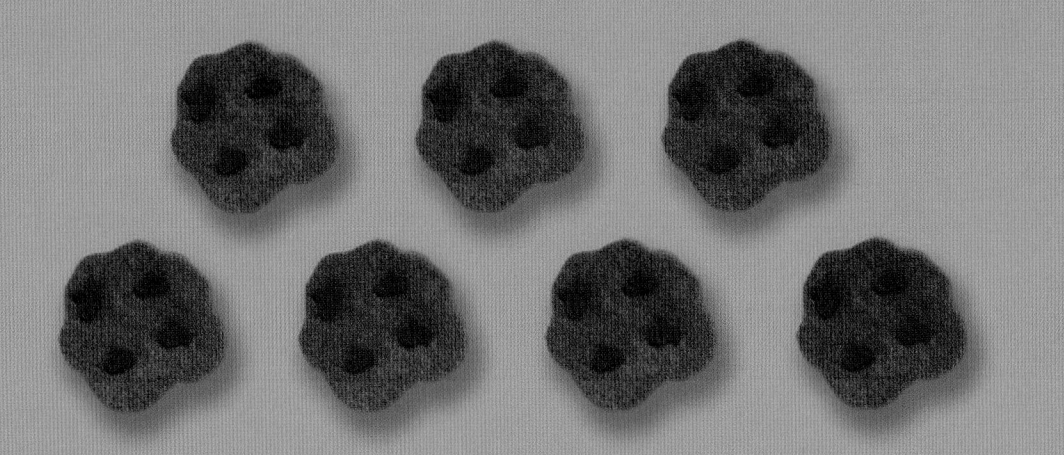

sept biscuits (seht bees-kwee)
seven cookies

6

SIX (sees)

Six is six.
Fun, colorful bouncy balls
to play with and to kick.

six balles (sees bahl)
six balls

5

CINQ (saNk)

Cinq is five.
Count the bumble bees
buzzin' around the hive.

cinq abeilles (saNk kah-beh-y)
five bees

4 QUATRE (kahtr)

Quatre is four.
Crunchy, red apples
eaten to the core.

quatre pommes (kahtr pohm)
four apples

3

TROIS (trwah)

Trois is three.
Listen to the lovely birds
singing in the tree.

trois oiseaux (trwah zwah-zoh)
three birds

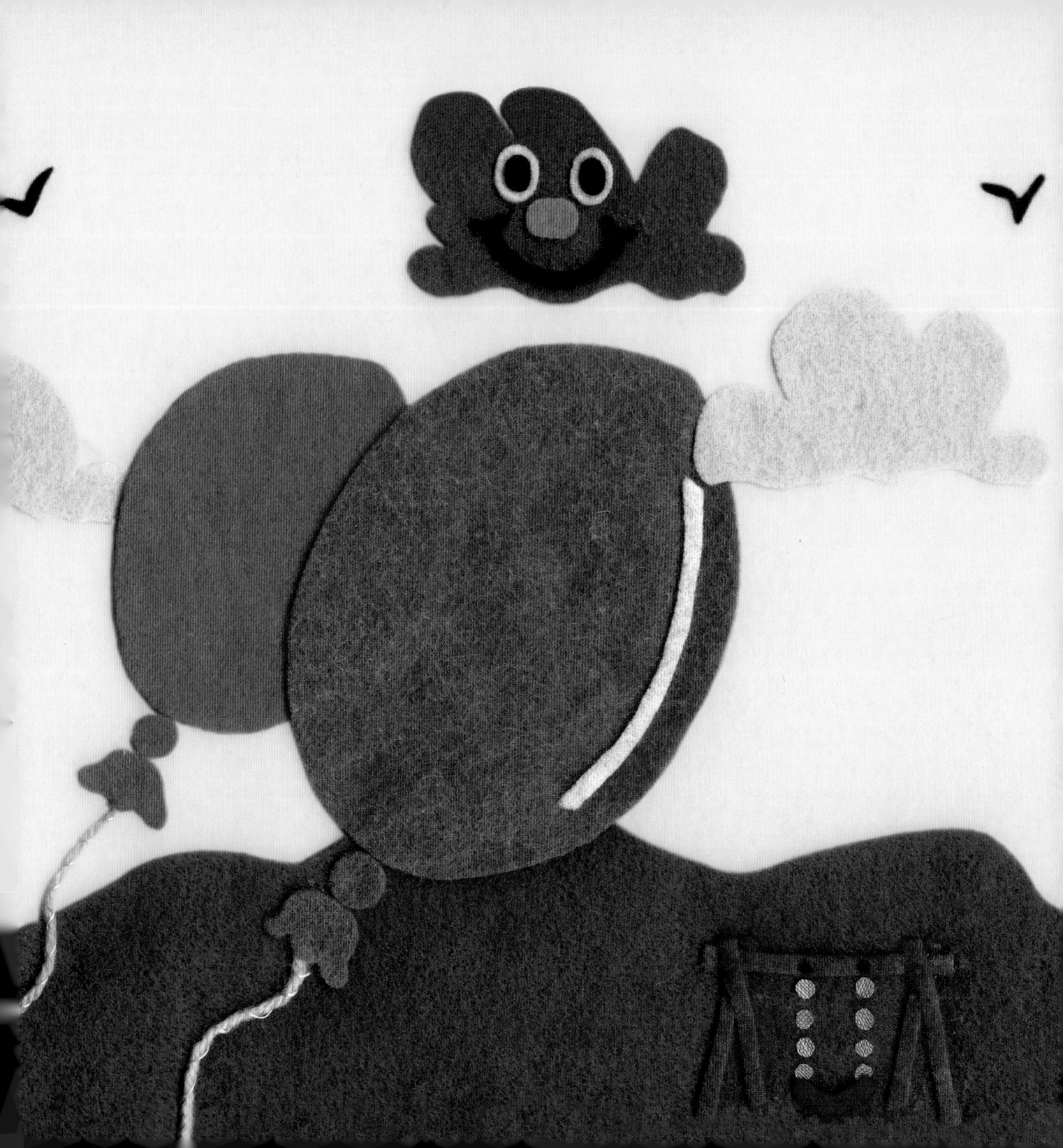

2

DEUX (duh)

Deux is two.
Oh, no! Catch the balloons,
they're floating out of view.

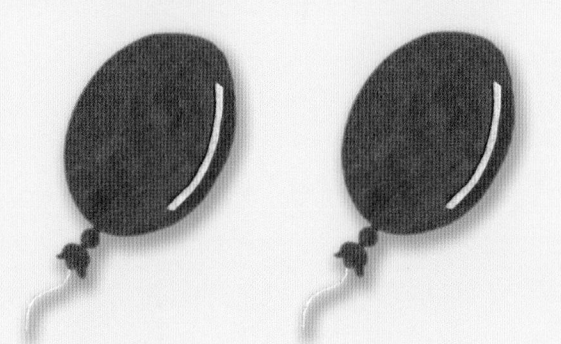

deux ballons (duh bah-lohN)
two balloons

1

UN (uhN)

Un is one.
A rhythmic, wooden drum to
beat on just for fun.

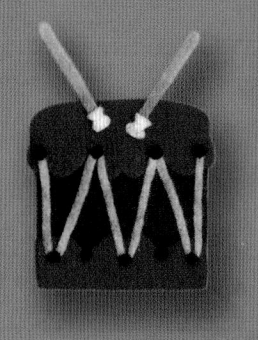

un tambour (uhN tahN-boor)
one drum

ChatterWorld
playdates for little linguists™

My Numbers in French

Mes nombres en français

Zakiyyah

Little Linguists Press